W9-BCQ-815

The Adventures of Salt and Soap

WRITTEN BY Lori April Rome
ILLUSTRATED BY Tim Jessell

Grand Canyon Association

Grand Canyon Association
PO Box 399, Grand Canyon, AZ 86023
800/858-2808
www.grandcanyon.org

Text © 2017 by Lori April Rome
Illustrations © 2017 by Tim Jessell

All Rights Reserved. No portion of this book may be reproduced in whole or in part, by any means (with the exception of short quotes for the purpose of review), without permission of the publisher.

Composed in the United States of America

Printed by WeSP Co. In., Seoul, South Korea
Production Date 03.08.17
Batch# 78959-0

Edited by Theresa Howell
Design by David Jenney Design

First Edition 2009
New Revised Edition 2017
ISBN 978-1-934656-69-3

20 19 18 17 1 2 3 4

Library of Congress Cataloging-in-Publication Data Pending

Author's Acknowledgement

Thanks to everyone who cared for Salt and Soap during their adventures at Grand Canyon and around the world throughout their amazing lives. My deepest gratitude goes to Grand Canyon, the place where I met the furry loves of my life, which will forever be a place of inspiration, wonder, and adventure. Thanks and love to Kevin, to baby brother Morri, and of course my girls, Salt and Soap.

Grand Canyon Association

As the National Park Service's official nonprofit partner, Grand Canyon Association provides private funding to enable Grand Canyon National Park to raise the margin of excellence for educational programs and preservation, build innovation in Park services, and support the necessities not currently funded by federal dollars. Proceeds from the sale of this book directly support this purpose.

For more information on the Grand Canyon Association or to become a supporter, visit www.grandcanyon.org.

For Salt and Soap,
who make life an adventure and bring joy to the world.
Their story is dedicated to rescued dogs everywhere
and the people who adopt and love them.

—L. R.

Under a brilliant blue sky,

a cottontail hides in the brush, while a coyote waits patiently to make chase. A raven soars overhead. Red earth carpets the ground of this warm Arizona wilderness on the eastern rim of Grand Canyon.

Everything looks exactly as it should, *except*...for two puppies, napping side by side. Their paws wiggle and their whiskers twitch as dreams of adventure fill their sleepy heads.

The scent of sagebrush catches the wind and a distant noise awakens the pups.

"Where did you two come from?" the National Park Service rangers ask, surprised to see puppies in such a remote area of the park. Parks are for wild animals, not puppies, but the pups don't know that. They roll over and wiggle with excitement as the rangers rub their bellies.

The pups peer over the rim to watch as their new friends start down the trail on their way to meet some river rangers at the bottom of the canyon. They want to go too! They bound down the canyon's steep slopes after the rangers. Together they all hike deeper and deeper into Grand Canyon National Park.

By sunset, the rangers and pups reach the Colorado River. Red, pink, and orange rock walls tower above them.

"I can't believe these brave puppies made it down to the bottom!" a river ranger exclaims.

The puppies squeal with delight and greet them with yips and licks.

All these new friends!

After dinner, the dogs curl up on a ranger's raft and quickly fall asleep, until... Plip...plop...plip...plop. Rain splashes onto the ground.

Boom!

Thunder shakes the pups' raft, and lightning streaks above.

Frightened, the puppies jump off the boat, dash into a tent, and snuggle up next to a ranger.

In the morning, the river rangers get ready to continue their trip. The puppies wag their tails, hoping to go along with them.

"Sorry, girls. The river is too dangerous for puppies," they say.

"How about a treat?" offers one of the park rangers, heading back up the trail. "Let's get you back to the rim."

The puppies follow the rangers all the way to the top.

"Go on home," they say, pointing to the houses off in the distance.

But the pups want to go on another adventure. They peer down the trail at the river far below. After the rangers are gone, they head back into the canyon.

A dozen miles upriver, a group of friends launches their raft for the journey of a lifetime. As they float down the Colorado River they see many amazing things. Bighorn sheep drink along the riverbanks and scavenging California condors circle overhead, searching for meals.

Suddenly, they see something even more amazing.

What on earth are puppies doing at the bottom of Grand Canyon? they wonder.

The river runners offer the dogs food, water, and lots of attention. They even give them names!

"Let's call the white one Salt after Salt Water Wash!"

"How about Soap for the black and brown one, after the nearby side canyon?" another river runner suggests.

"Salt and Soap it is!" they exclaim.

It's too hot and dangerous to keep the puppies, so the river runners decide to take them to safety at the ranger station at Phantom Ranch, eighty miles downriver.

Splash! Swoosh! Crashing rapids toss the boats around in the river.

"Hold on!" the river runners shout.

POW! SLAM! A huge wave hits, and the raft flips. Pups and people tumble into the icy, cold water. The water pulls them under, then spits them back out. Both the pups and the river runners struggle to swim to shore.

Safe and sound at last, the river runners and pups cozy up with blankets, towels, and hot drinks. They are overjoyed to be dry and warm. Everyone settles in for a good night's sleep in order to be ready to continue their journey to Phantom Ranch.

A few days later, farther down the river at Phantom Ranch, the morning begins like any other. The rangers hike, watch for wildlife, and talk to hikers about nature, *until…*

Knock, knock.

Ranger Lori opens the ranger station door and finds quite a surprise.

"Oh my goodness, puppies!" she laughs.

After hearing the story of how Salt and Soap got to the bottom of Grand Canyon, Ranger Lori takes them in as lost and found items. The pups bark and yip their good-byes as the river runners head back to their rafts.

"I've got work to do," says Ranger Lori. "And until we can find a way to get you pups out of the canyon, I guess you'll have to join me."

Adorned with blue bandanas, rope leashes, and Junior Ranger badges, the pups help check permits and make sure food is secured from wildlife at the campground. They wag their tails and make friends with the campers they meet.

At the end of the day, Ranger Lori explains to Salt and Soap that tomorrow their adventure will continue.

"Just wait and see," she tells them.

Whoosh, whoosh, whoosh!

"Here comes your ride!" Ranger Lori exclaims.

A helicopter zooms into view and lands in the narrow canyon near Phantom Ranch. The crewmembers place helmets on the pups' heads before they climb into their kennels.

"Hang on!" the pilot warns. "This will be a quick eight-minute trip!"

Canyon walls drop away as the helicopter rises high into the sky. Soon, the river looks like a watery thread.

OPEN

N368PA
NPS
NATIONAL PARK SERVICE

Once in the South Rim forest, Salt and Soap find a new home on the edge of Grand Canyon with Ranger Lori. They have a big yard, where elk and deer pass by and squirrels eat pinecones in the tree branches above. They hide whenever thunderstorms boom overhead.

Never apart for a day in their lives, Salt and Soap nap in the summer sun, side-by-side, safe and loved. Their paws and ears twitch as they dream of what their next adventure might be.

Epilogue

Salt and Soap have had the great fortune of enjoying life to the fullest, side by side. In 2003, they entered the world, and together, the adventure began. In 2011, their younger brother Morri, a three-legged rescue from Capitol Reef National Park, joined the pack. They have camped, hiked, sniffed, and explored in deserts, forests, prairies, and mountains; along oceans, rivers, and lakes. They rafted down the Colorado River in Grand Canyon National Park, traveled across the entire United States, and explored numerous national park sites and other public lands. They even crossed the Atlantic Ocean on the Queen Mary 2 ocean liner, all the way to Europe. The pack walked on coastlines in England, frolicked in Germany's Black Forest, and strutted down the promenade at the Eiffel Tower in Paris. After their 18-month European adventure, they returned to enjoying sunsets at home on the Colorado Plateau once again. After a long dog walk, wherever that might be, the best part of the adventure is snuggling together as a pack at the end of each day. Family comes in many shapes and sizes. Family is love, and love has been the best adventure and the greatest gift of this life.